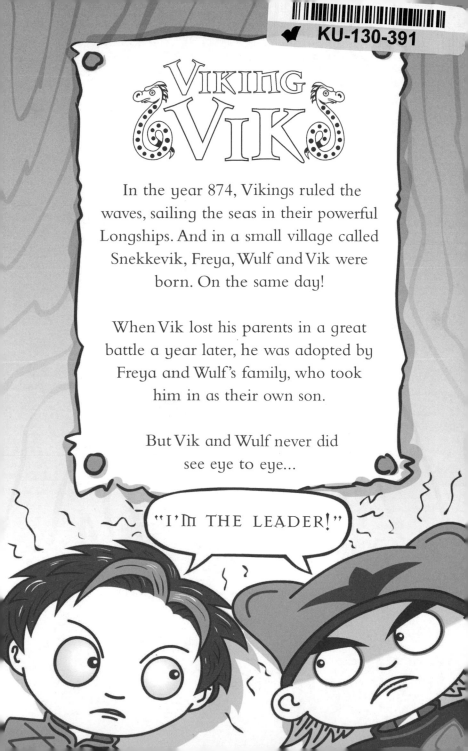

VIKING VIK

In the year 874, Vikings ruled the waves, sailing the seas in their powerful Longships. And in a small village called Snekkevik, Freya, Wulf and Vik were born. On the same day!

When Vik lost his parents in a great battle a year later, he was adopted by Freya and Wulf's family, who took him in as their own son.

But Vik and Wulf never did see eye to eye...

"I'M THE LEADER!"

FOR

TANTE NILLA

First published in 2008 by Orchard Books
First paperback publication in 2009

ORCHARD BOOKS
338 Euston Road, London NW1 3BH
Orchard Books Australia
Level 17/207 Kent St, Sydney, NSW 2000

ISBN 978 1 84616 723 2 (hardback)
ISBN 978 1 84616 731 7 (paperback)

Text and illustrations © Shoo Rayner 2008

The right of Shoo Rayner to be identified as the author and
illustrator of this work has been asserted by him in accordance with the
Copyright, Designs and Patents Act, 1988.

A CIP catalogue record for this book is available from the British Library.

1 3 5 7 9 10 8 6 4 2 (hardback)
1 3 5 7 9 10 8 6 4 2 (paperback)

Printed in Great Britain by Antony Rowe Ltd, Chippenham, Wiltshire

Orchard Books is a division of Hachette Children's Books,
an Hachette Livre UK company.

www.hachettelivre.co.uk

VIKING VIK

AND THE BIG FIGHT

SHOO RAYNER

ORCHARD BOOKS

"I'm the leader!" Vik yelled, thrusting his wooden sword towards the sky.

"No, you're not!" Wulf snarled. "I'm the leader!"

Wulf bounded up the sharp ridge of the Dragon Rock. The two boys stared into each other's eyes. There was no great love between them. Wulf pulled a wooden club from his belt and swung at Vik.

Vik ducked, swung
his sword and caught
Wulf a glancing blow
on the arm.

"Now you've done it,"
Wulf hissed. "I'll show
you who's the leader."

Wulf leapt on top of Vik. The two boys grappled and slid down the side of the rock into the gritty dust below.

They punched, they bit, they pinched and they kicked.

Vik's dog, Flek, yapped and barked and tried to help his master.

8

THE DRAGON ROCK

The Dragon Rock, on the beach at Snekkevik, is really *two* rocks. They look like the head and body of a dragon that is half-buried in the sand. Children have always met and played on the Dragon Rock. They pretend they're flying on the dragon's back, or they just play "King of the Castle".

"Stop!" shouted Freya. "Why do you two always have to fight?" She grabbed her brothers and tried to pull them apart. "For Odin's sake, will you please stop it!"

Wulf lashed out, hoping to silence Vik for good.

Freya's piercing scream stopped both boys in their tracks. Freya's hands were pressed to her face. She glared at Wulf. Tears fell from her brown eyes, which flashed with the anger burning inside her.

"I'm sorry, Freya," Wulf began. "I didn't think, I just…"

Freya pulled her hands away from her mouth. Blood trickled from her bottom lip.

"You never think!" she snapped back at him.

The two boys hung their heads in shame.

"Are you all right, Freya?" Vik asked.

Freya explored her swollen lip with her tongue and checked that she still had all her teeth. "Le-le-le — I suppose," she mumbled.

But Freya was angry. She put her hands on her hips and told the two boys exactly what she thought of them.

"You're pathetic! You're always fighting to be the leader. Well, it takes more than strength to be a leader. It takes courage and brains, too.

"You should have a competition to decide who the leader is once and for all."

"Hey! That's a really good idea," said Wulf.

"What sort of competition did you have in mind?" Vik asked, cautiously.

"I'll think of something," said Freya.

COMPETITIONS

Vikings love competitions
to decide who is the...

...fiercest

...strongest

...greediest   ...and the meanest.

"How about
a running race?"
Vik suggested.

"You're easily
the fastest," Freya
replied. "It would
be unfair."

"How about a swimming race?" said Wulf.

"You've got such big feet, you swim like a dolphin," Freya laughed. "That would be unfair, too."

Suddenly Freya clapped her hands. "I know! You shall have an eating competition."

"Mmmmmm!" The boys rubbed their stomachs. "That sounds good," they chimed together.

"OK, that's what we'll do." Freya smiled secretly to herself. "I'll make the rules and choose what you eat."

"O-o-o-K…" The boys were suspicious, but they couldn't say no to Freya, not while her lip was still swollen and lumpy.

"I'll go and get everything ready. Meet back here later, and no fighting!" Freya ordered.

It was late
afternoon before
Freya was ready. She
placed six bowls, in
two rows of three, on
the Dragon Rock.

The bowls had lids so the boys couldn't see what was inside. Flek sniffed them with great interest.

"You have to swallow a whole mouthful and show me your empty mouth," Freya explained. "If you're sick afterwards, that's OK."

"Sick?!" Wulf yelped. "What do you want us to eat?"

Freya handed them a bowl each. Then, with a flourish, she whisked the lids off and announced, "Eel jelly!"

DISGUSTING THINGS TO EAT

Vikings don't have freezers, so most of the food in their larders is a little bit mouldy...

Mouldy
sheep's heads.

Old, sour, mouldy
goat's milk.

Soft, mouldy
goose fat.

Hard, dried,
mouldy bread.

"Urrrrrrgh!" The boys stared at the
cold, shimmering, green-grey, wobbling
mess in their bowls. Flek looked disgusted.
He ran away to find something nice to eat.

"Do we have to?" Wulf whined.

Vik looked at Freya's lip. This wasn't just about who became the leader – the honour of both the boys was at stake.

Vik took a handful of the jelly and put it in his mouth. It was the most revolting thing he had ever tasted. He tried to swallow but his stomach wouldn't let him. Vik closed his eyes and relaxed. The jelly slid down his throat as if it were live eels wriggling their way down a river.

Vik opened his empty mouth and
Freya clapped her hands.

"Well done!"
she said, as Vik
shuddered
violently.

As Vik lay on the ground retching, Wulf cleared his throat.

"Mmmm! That was delicious!"

He threw back his head and showed Freya his empty mouth and clean bowl.

"Your stomach must be made of iron," Freya said, suspiciously.

Freya handed out the bowls for the next challenge. "Try eating these…"

"Worms!" Vik felt sick already. "We don't have to eat them all, do we?"

"No. You only have to eat one," Freya explained, smiling sweetly, if a bit lopsidedly.

Wulf was winning. Vik
knew he needed to be really
brave. He chose the cleanest
worm, closed his eyes and
put it in his mouth.

"You don't
have to chew,"
said Freya.

This time he really could feel the worm wriggling in his throat as it slithered into his stomach. He showed Freya his empty mouth, then fell to the ground, choking and gagging.

"Mmmm! That was delicious!" Wulf boasted. "What's for pudding?" He had emptied his bowl once again!

Like a magician performing a trick, Freya lifted the lids off their last bowls.

Vik's stomach churned. Shiny balls of frogspawn, like a hundred tiny eyeballs, stared coldly at him from his bowl.

He couldn't let Wulf win. He scooped up a handful and put them in his mouth.

He shook his head and fought the revolting, slimy, sloppy balls down into his stomach.

Freya clapped her hands. "Well done, Vik! You can be sick now!"

"Mmmm! That was delicious!" Wulf threw his empty bowl on the floor and leapt onto the Dragon Rock. "I ate more than Vik and I wasn't sick, either. That makes me the winner!"

Vik lay in the dirt. His stomach
ached and his throat burned. A revolting
taste lingered in his mouth. He fought to
keep the tears away. It was so unfair. He
had eaten everything but had still lost.

Through his tears he watched Wulf march up and down the Dragon Rock, preening himself like a peacock, a smug grin plastered on his face. But there was something about Wulf's stomach…it moved in a mysterious, gloopy way. Vik remembered a story about Thor who tricked a dragon in an eating contest.

Had Wulf had done the same – had he tricked Vik and Freya?

THE STORY OF THOR AND THE DRAGON

The great god, Thor, had an eating competition with a dragon. Thor filled a leather bag with porridge and hid it under his jerkin.

When Thor was full, he cut the bag open with a knife. Porridge oozed out of his stomach! "I'm making room for more food," he said.

When the dragon realised that Thor could "empty his stomach", it gave up. Thor won the competition.

"You cheat!" Vik snarled.

Wulf stared blankly as Vik scrambled up the rock and flew at him. Vik grappled with Wulf's belt and pulled until the buckle broke. There was a horrible, squidgy, slurping noise, then Wulf groaned as eel jelly, worms and frogspawn slid slowly down the top of his trousers.

Wulf had poured the disgusting food down his leather jerkin while Freya was watching Vik being sick. He had remembered the story of Thor, too.

Now the revolting mess slipped down the insides of his trouser legs and into his boots.

Holding himself as if he'd wet his
pants, Wulf skulked back to the village
to clean himself up.

"You were so brave, eating all that
revolting stuff," Freya told Vik. "I didn't
think you'd really do it, you know."

"I had to," Vik explained. "After Wulf hit you, it was the only way to regain our honour. And Wulf still cheated!"

Vik watched the pathetic figure of Wulf as he delicately picked his way home.

Vik stood tall on the
Dragon Rock. "You'll
never be the leader!" he
called after Wulf. "You
haven't got the guts!"

SHOO RAYNER

All priced at £8.99

The Viking Vik stories are available from all good bookshops,
or can be ordered direct from the publisher:
Orchard Books, PO BOX 29, Douglas IM99 1BQ
Credit card orders please telephone 01624 836000
or fax 01624 837033 or visit our internet site: www.orchardbooks.co.uk
or e-mail: bookshop@enterprise.net for details.

To order please quote title, author and ISBN
and your full name and address.
Cheques and postal orders should be made payable to 'Bookpost plc.'
Postage and packing is FREE within the UK
(overseas customers should add £2.00 per book).

Prices and availability are subject to change.